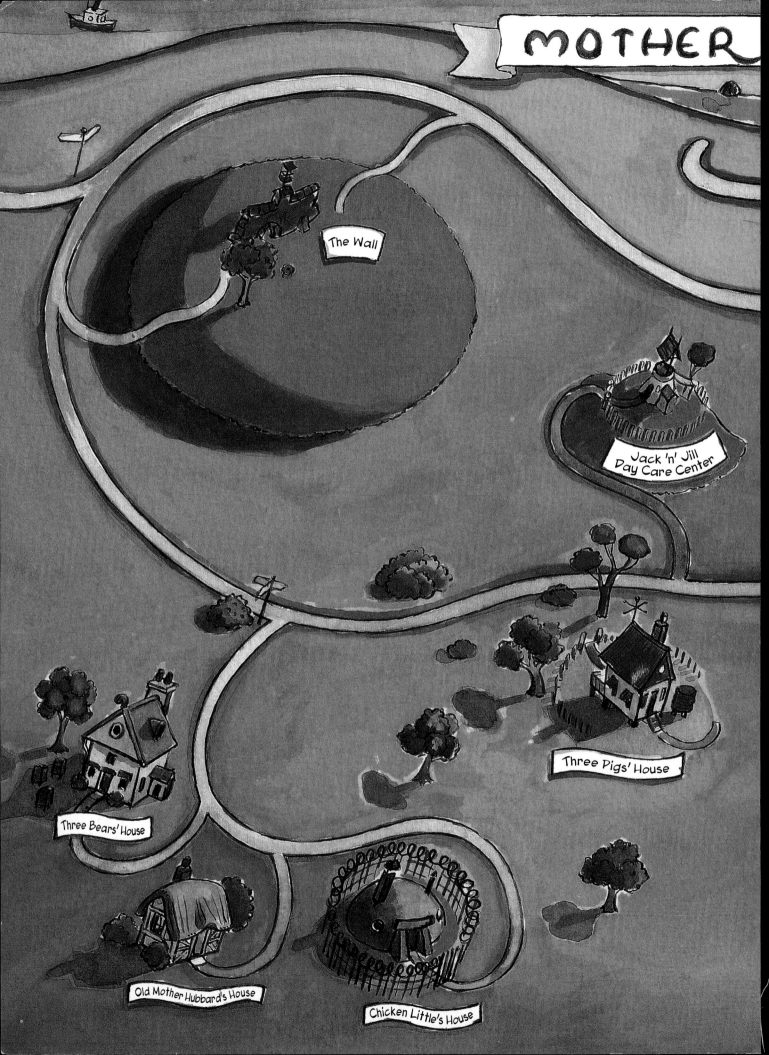

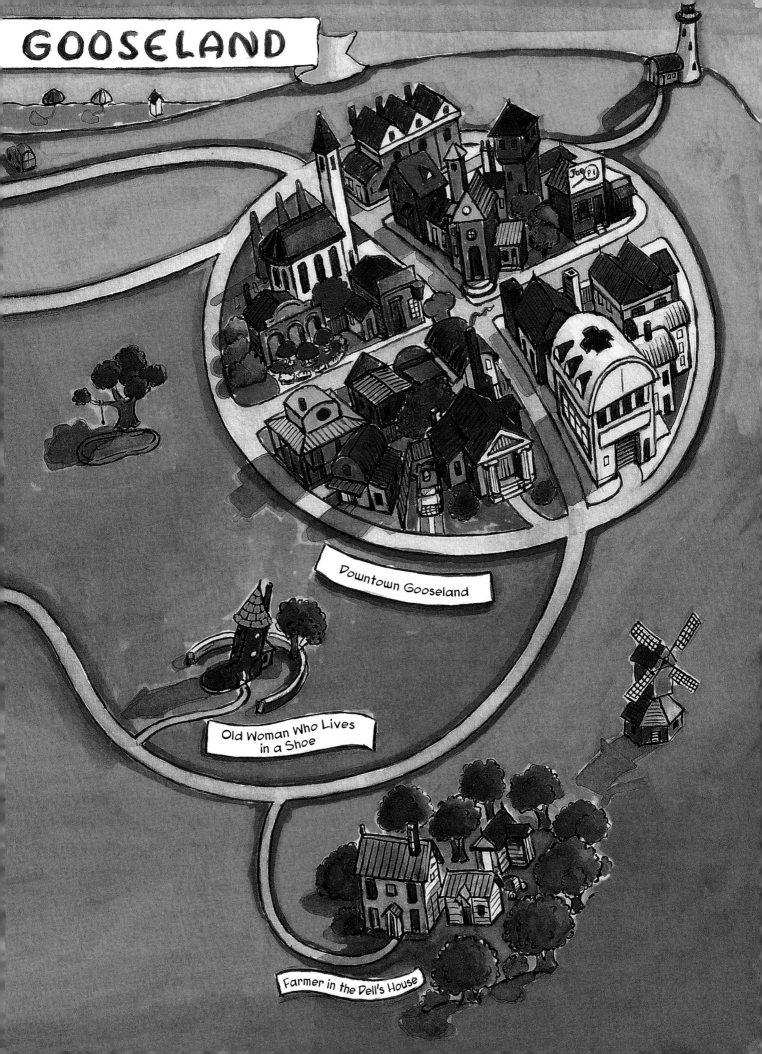

What REALLY Happened to Humpty?

(from the files of a hard-boiled detective)

by
Joe Dumpty

as told to
Jeanie Franz Ransom

illustrated by
Stephen Axelsen

ini Charlesbridge

For my egg-cellent editor, Randi, and Aunt Kris
—J. F. R.

For Joey, a good egg
—S. A.

Published by Charlesbridge
85 Main Street
Watertown, MA 02472
(617) 926-0329
www.charlesbridge.com

Library of Congress Cataloging-in-Publication Data
Ransom, Jeanie Franz, 1957–
    What really happened to Humpty? : from the files of a hard-boiled detective /
as told to Jeanie Franz Ransom ; illustrated by Stephen Axelsen.
        p. cm.
    Summary: Detective Joe Dumpty rushes to investigate the mysterious
circumstances under which his older brother, Humpty, fell from a wall on
his first day as captain of the new Neighborhood Watch program.
    ISBN 978-1-58089-109-7 (reinforced for library use)
    ISBN 978-1-58089-391-6 (softcover)
    ISBN 978-1-60734-103-1 (ebook pdf)
[1. Characters in literature—Fiction. 2. Mystery and detective stories.
3. Humorous stories.] I. Axelsen, Stephen, ill. II. Title.
PZ7.R1744Whd 2009
[E]—dc22   2008007232

Printed in China
(hc) 10 9 8 7 6 5 4 3 2
(sc) 10

Illustrations done in watercolor and pen and ink on Canson Montval 300 gsm paper
Display type and text type set in Typeka Mix, American Typewriter, and Blambot Pro
Color separations by Chroma Graphics, Singapore
Printed by Jade Productions in Heyuan, Guangdong, China
Production supervision by Brian G. Walker
Designed by Diane M. Earley

Humpty Dumpty sat on a wall.
Humpty Dumpty had a great fall.
Humpty Dumpty was pushed.

At least I think so. Who am I? I'm Joe Dumpty,
Humpty's younger brother.

You probably haven't heard of me. I never was Mother's favorite. Mother Goose, that is. Ever since she became Police Chief Goose, she thinks I'm just stirring up trouble with my detective business.

Yes, Mother Goose always liked Humpty best. He's such a good egg. That's why I think it's a crime that he fell off the Wall. After all, he'd been sitting up there for as long as I can remember with no problems whatsoever. Until that awful, scrambled-up day.

It was a picture-book-perfect morning. The Old Woman
Who Lives in a Shoe had just dropped off her kids at
the Jack 'n' Jill Day Care Center. The Three Little Pigs
were putting the finishing touches on their latest house.
And across the field, Humpty was sitting on the Wall.

I wish I'd stopped to crack a few jokes with my brother—but
it was Humpty's first week as captain of our new Neighborhood
Watch program, and I didn't want to distract him.

Besides, it was almost nine, and I had to get to work.

I made a quick stop and ran into Little Red Riding Hood.

"The Muffin Man's scrambling to fill a big order,"
Red said. "I can't even buy one lousy muffin for my
grandmother!" She sniffed loudly and stomped off in a huff.

With my espresso in hand, I headed to the office.

As I opened my office door, the phone rang. It was Little Miss Muffet. "Joe, something's happened to Humpty!"

I raced to the Wall. Miss Muffet was there, cell phone
in hand. "I called 911," she sobbed.

I looked at my brother. He wasn't making a sound.
Whoever did this was gonna fry!

I walked back around the Wall, and that's when I saw it.
Something shiny was tucked under Miss Muffet's tuffet.
She was on the phone, so I didn't bother asking if I could
look under her tuffet. I just did.

Sometimes detectives have to
act first and ask questions later.

It was a pair of binoculars. Not just any binoculars. These puppies were the Official Binoculars of the Neighborhood Watch program. Humpty had been showing them off ever since he'd become captain.

Were you looking under my tuffet?

"What are you doing with those?" Muffy asked, grabbing the binoculars. I was just about to ask her the same thing, when . . .

. . . all the king's horses and all the king's men
arrived. They couldn't put Humpty together again,
so they scooped him up and rushed to the hospital.

"What's the story?" I asked Muffy. I wanted some answers.
Muffy sighed. "I was just shooting the breeze with Humpty,
waiting for Spider. Humpty was letting me try his binoculars
when suddenly this huffy-puffy wind blew him right off the Wall!"

Police Chief Goose pulled up in her big honking cruiser. "I was at the Three Pigs'," she apologized. "The wind we had this morning blew down their new house."

"I just told Joe that the wind made Humpty fall," Muffy said.

"*I* made Humpty fall," said a small voice out of nowhere.

"It's my fault," Spider said, dropping down from the tree. "I was rushing to get down here by nine this morning—my usual time—when this puff of wind pushed me straight toward Humpty. I must have scared him, because the next thing I knew, Humpty was on the ground. I zipped home, but I knew I had to 'fess up. Humpty was my friend."

"My brother wasn't afraid of anything! That's why he was the perfect Neighborhood Watch captain. What happened to Humpty wasn't your fault, Spider," I said.

"It wasn't anybody's fault," Muffy chimed in. "It was an accident."

"Agreed," Chief Goose said. "Go on to the hospital, Joe," she told me. "I'll write up an accident report."

"But Chief, Humpty's been sitting on the Wall for years without a wobble," I said. "Then the first week he's Neighborhood Watch captain, he suddenly falls off? The same day the Pigs' house blows down? Coincidence? I don't think so."

Chief Goose sighed. "OK, Joe, since Humpty's your brother, I'll give you 'til five o'clock to play detective. If you don't have anything by then, I'm writing that accident report."

I didn't have much time. I hurried to the hospital.
Thanks to the miracles of modern technology, combined
with some nifty techniques the doctors discovered when
Jack fell down and broke his crown, Humpty was on the
mend. But he didn't remember a thing. I needed to hit
the streets and question a few characters myself.

My first stop was the Bears'. I rang the doorbell three times and was about to give up when the door opened to reveal a bare foot. I was expecting a *bear* foot!

I showed the blonde my badge and asked about the Bears' whereabouts. "I'm house-sitting," she said, yawning.

"Late night?" I asked.

"Early morning. Some dog started howling and woke me up."

"How early?" I probed.

"Nine AM," she said. "But now that I'm awake, want to come in for some porridge?"

I hated to tell her no, but I was on the clock. And that clock was ticking.

Next house I visited belonged to the only dog owner in the neighborhood, Old Mother Hubbard. Maybe her pup had been howling this morning. But Mrs. H. said, "I gave my dog to the Farmer in the Dell last week. He needed help with his sheep, and unlike mine, his cupboard is never bare."

Mrs. H. shook her head sadly when I told her about Humpty. "I never would have done anything to Humpty, not even to feed my poor dog.

"Maybe you should talk to my neighbor," Mrs. H. added. "She seemed to be in a big hurry this morning."

Chicken Little answered the door looking more nervous than usual. "Am I in t-t-trouble?"

I played it cool. "You tell me," I said, keeping a close eye on her in case she tried to fly the coop.

"If it's about what happened this morning, it's not my fault," Chicken Little said.

"You know what happened this morning?"

"Of course I know!" she shouted. "The sky fell! And I didn't warn anyone. I've learned to keep my beak shut."

"The sky didn't fall this morning," I said. "Humpty did." From her surprised look, I knew she was innocent. "He's going to be OK," I said.

"I love that egg like he's one of my own," Chicken Little sniffled. I handed the tender chicken a tissue.

"So tell me where you were around nine," I said.

"I was on my morning power walk," she answered. "I'd just passed Muffy and Humpty when the wind howled overhead. I'd just walked behind the Wall, and the next thing I knew, the sky—I mean Humpty—was falling. I ran straight home."

"Was Humpty sitting on the Wall when you saw him?"

"Yes, but Muffy wasn't sitting on her tuffet." Chicken Little paused. "That's funny . . . she's usually digging into her curds and whey."

Funny indeed.

As I left my friend clucking to herself and scanning the sky, I heard a commotion coming from the Pigs' house—what was left of it, anyway.

Huff, puff, huff, puff. *I need more exercise*, I thought as I raced across the field. How many times had I heard people say that today? Not the "more exercise" part— the "huff, puff" part, as in "a huffy-puffy wind."

I found the Pigs fighting over, of all things, a cell phone. I thought everyone had one these days. Apparently not.

"OK, guys, hand it over," I said. "Whose phone is this?"

"We don't know," the pigs said. "We found it this morning after our house blew down."

Just then the phone rang. Actually, it howled. Who would have a howl for a ring tone? I took a guess and disguised my voice. "Yo," I growled.

"I got the binoculars," the voice on the phone said. "Now I want my yummy-wummy muffins. We had a deal, remember? Be at the Wall in five minutes."

I called Chief Goose and told her to meet me at the Wall.
The clues were adding up—the muffins that no one else
could buy, the howling that didn't come from a dog,
the huffy-puffy wind. Not to mention the binoculars that
someone wanted—bad! But why? I had a hunch.

Muffy was at the Wall, binoculars in hand. She didn't look too happy to see me. "Expecting someone else?" I asked. "Someone big and bad perhaps?"

"She's expecting me!" howled the Big Bad Wolf as he jumped out and grabbed the binoculars.

"Where are my muffins?" screamed Muffy. "I'm sick of curds and whey!"

"Sorry, doll, plan's changed," growled Wolf.

"You pushed Humpty off the Wall," I said. "I'm telling Chief Goose."

"I wasn't at the Wall this morning," Wolf said.

"But you *were* at the Pigs' house," I said, showing Wolf his phone. "When you blew down their house, you got Humpty, too. Guess you wanted a scrambled egg with your bacon."

"Wolf just wanted the binoculars," Muffy cried.
"He promised me some yummy-wummy muffins if I'd get them from Humpty. No one was supposed to get hurt!"

"And nobody else will, if you give me my phone, Joe, and get out of my way," Wolf snarled.

My, what big teeth he has, I thought. Where was Chief Goose?

"Hold it," shrieked Spider.

"What's going on here?" Chief Goose had arrived.

"It seems that the howling wind this morning was actually Wolf blowing down the Pigs' new house—and Humpty along with it," I told the chief. "That's my theory, anyway."

"What about Muffy?" Chief asked.

"Actually, it's a conspiracy theory," I said. "Wolf promised our Little Miss muffins in exchange for Humpty's binoculars. Without the binoculars Humpty couldn't see Wolf blow down the Pigs' house."

"Apparently Wolf also threatened to blow down the Muffin Man's shop unless he got free muffins," Chief Goose said. "The guy's been hiding in a sack of sugar all day."

"Sweet," Wolf snarled.

Muffy glared at him. "I wouldn't have helped you if I'd known the truth. Humpty was my friend. Now he'll probably never speak to me again."

"You can always call him from your cell to apologize," I told her. "Your jail cell, that is."

"So, why'd you do it, Wolf?"
I asked.

"I'm Bad," he said,
shrugging his shoulders.
"It's my middle name."

"I have to hand it to you,
Joe," Chief Goose said, "you
were right. What happened to
Humpty really was a crime.
You weren't afraid to trust
your gut and get to the bottom
of this. I'm proud of you, Joe."

I have to admit, I was proud of me, too. And of my brave friend Spider. In fact, Spider's the Neighborhood Watch captain while Humpty's healing. As for me . . .

I've had plenty of cases to solve—dozens of 'em, in fact. Word on the street is the Dish ran away with the Spoon. And then there's my friend Bo. Bo Peep, that is. That dame keeps me in business. Now, if I were a sheep, where would I go?

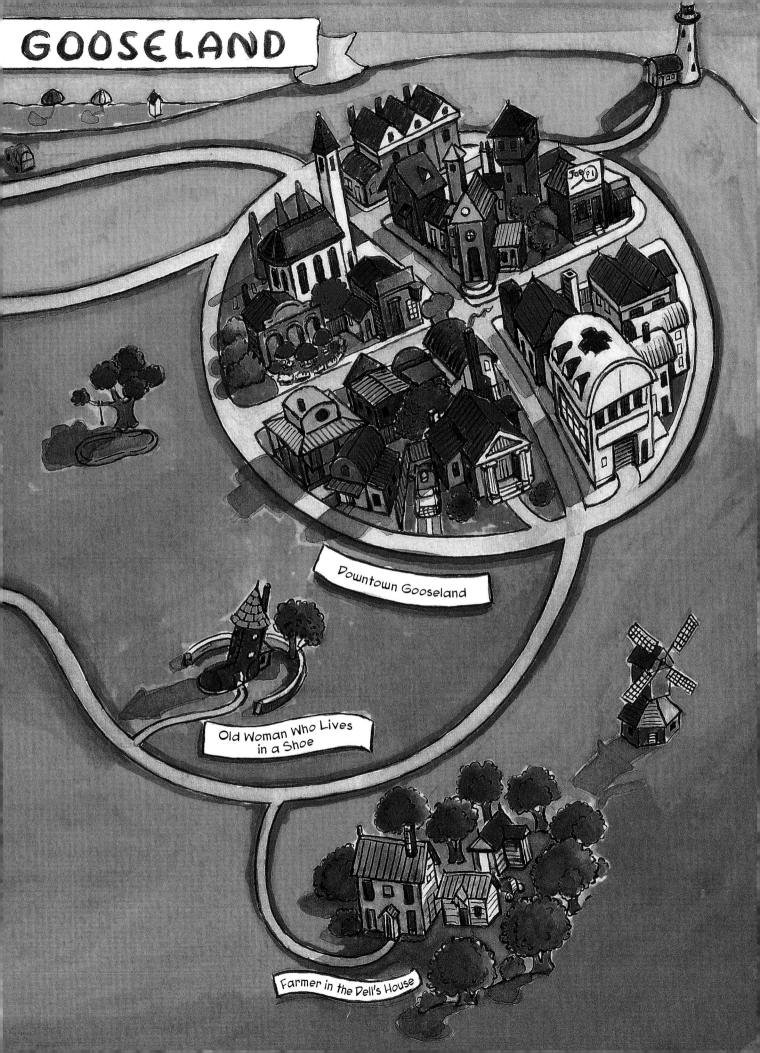